SINGULARITY SUN

SINGULARITY SUN

A CIARÁN MAC DIARMUID STORY

FREEMAN UNIVERSE
BOOK 4.5

PATRICK O'SULLIVAN

dunkerron press

A Dunkerron Press™ Book.

Copyright © 2022 by Patrick O'Sullivan

PatrickOSullivan.com

ISBN-13: 978-1-62560-031-8

ISBN-10: 1-62560-031-3

All rights reserved. Except for use in any review, the reproduction or utilization of this work in whole or in part in any form by an electronic, mechanical or other means, now known or hereafter invented, including xerography, photocopying and recording, or in any information storage or retrieval system, is forbidden without the written permission of the publisher, Dunkerron Press, P.O. Box 501180, Marathon FL 33050-1180.

This is a work of fiction. Names, characters, dialogue, places and incidents are either the product of the author's imagination or are used fictitiously, and any resemblance to actual persons, living or dead, business establishments, events or locales is entirely coincidental.

Dunkerron Press and the Dunkerron colophon are trademarks of Dunkerron, LLC.

BOOKS IN THIS SERIES

Novels:

Quite Possibly Alien

Quite Possibly Allies

Quite Possibly Heroes

Quite Possibly Final

Impossibly Alien

Novellas, Novelettes, and Short Story Collections:

Quite Possibly True

Quite Possibly False

Singularity Sun

1

———————

They dropped anchor half a kilometer offshore. The sea lay smooth between the silt-clouded mouth of the Willow Bride's Tears and the ancient sailing sloop. The vessel looked its age, with lifelines slack, topsides worn, brightwork unvarnished and poorly maintained, the sails threadbare and mildewed. The engine ran rough when it ran. The present owner had been plying the star lanes for more than a local year, and before that, off-world at university for more than four. He could see the dock and the boat's slip from where he stood on the foredeck.

The measure of today's journey wasn't distance, but time.

No one expected a clear day like no one expected an answered prayer. And it was a clear day, the second clear day in a row, and while chilly in absolute terms, positively balmy as experienced locally.

The sun hung high in the sky, the sky utterly devoid of clouds, the not-too-distant shoreline clear and distinct, a rocky strand framing a small cove in the foreground, a haphazardly assembled farmstead upland, and behind it all the mountain.

A ruin of vessels crowded the little cove, the principal wreck a large and rusting self-powered barge. The level ground, where a tumbledown barn used to stand, now hosted a glass-field for longboats descending from orbit.

Perhaps three days such as this occurred every year or two. Oileán Chléire on most days lay shadowed beneath low scudding clouds, and if it didn't spit icy rain it wasn't winter, and if it didn't spit lukewarm rain it wasn't summer. The shoulder seasons might turn up anything; a low fog, a high fog, a soft rain, a hard rain, intermittent rain, continuous rain, rain mixed with hail, wet hail, hard hail, icy rain, sooty rain, when the prevailing winds blew from the east, and on a rare occasion such as today, a clear day.

Lorelei Ellis stood at the helm in a distracting two-piece bathing suit as she shifted the engine into reverse and backed down on the anchor. Satisfied with the set, she circled a single finger in the air and Ciarán snubbed the line tight. He owned a bathing suit as well, one he'd had since he was sixteen, and now fit him like it was sprayed on. Some things couldn't be planned for. No one expected a clear day.

Lorelei switched the engine off and came forward. She sprawled on the foredeck.

"You're pasty as a stationer," she said. "It's not a good look on you."

"I'm fixing to lobster up." He settled in beside her as the hull swung on anchor and settled.

"I don't think that's a good plan."

"Do you have a better one?"

"Always."

The boat had swung around so that the foredeck faced the shore. Ciarán stretched his legs out. "You know, when I dream it looks like this."

"You dream of being aboard an old wreck of a sailboat?"

"I don't. I mean the home place. It's always a clear day, and I think I could count those real days on the fingers of my hands, and not even need thumbs."

"Do you miss the barn?"

He contemplated the glassfield. "I don't miss mucking it out."

"Is it there in your dreams?"

"I don't recall. It's not something I note. The farmyard, the well, the turf bank, the riverside, the mountain. Mostly the river, and the willows, if it's a good dream."

"And if it's a nightmare?"

"The kitchen."

His mother had first fallen in the kitchen. She hadn't died there, but it felt like she had. It had been a long, drawn-out death. Six years ago, almost seven, and he carried it with him like it was yesterday.

"I don't dream," Lorelei said.

"Why not?"

"It feels dangerous." She glanced at him. "You are leaving me. You can say it."

"I'm not *leaving* you." He turned toward her. "What does that even mean?"

"Oh. I said that wrong. You're leaving. And I'm staying."

"I—"

She pressed a finger to his lips. "It's all good. Really." She reclined against the deckhouse. "Let's enjoy the sun while we have it."

Ciarán watched the shoreline. He had no intention of leaving Lorelei. He had no idea what had caused her to say that. He'd been home for nearly a month, and they'd been together day and night. "You're somewhat pasty yourself," he said.

"It's a good look on me."

Ciarán didn't say anything. Her skin white as milk, her hair a raven's wing brushing her shoulders, she stretched out on the deck, her profile limned like an artist's proof. If islanders minted coins, her likeness would stand proud upon its face.

She leaned on her elbow and watched his face with eyes the precise shade of willow bark. "Well?"

"I'm not disagreeing." It wasn't a good look on her. It was a fantastic look, but that wasn't something he wanted to say. She'd always been ethereal. Maybe she would look even better if she wasn't so pale. He tried imagining her with a tan. An all over tan, one without tan lines.

"Those are some tight swim trunks."

"It's not like there's a swimwear store nearby."

Lorelei chuckled. "I will miss you, Ciarán mac Diarmuid. You are so utterly clueless."

"It's entirely an act." Ciarán stood. "And I'm sticking."

Lorelei's attention turned westward. "We have company."

A small boat had come around the headland.

Ciarán shaded his eyes and peered into the distance. "Strangers, I take it." Lorelei had the eyesight of a hawk. He could make out the hull but little else. The sound of the distant motor arrived an instant before Lorelei spoke.

"Seems that way. Maybe you'll want to go below."

"And do what? Hide?" He was a somewhat wanted man, not for anything he'd done, but for a raft of things he knew and wasn't saying. He might prove easy prey out in the world, but only a fool would come after him at home.

"Too late. They've seen you."

The boat was an inflatable skiff, black hull, black outboard power, three men aboard. They crossed the delta of the Willow Bride on a plane and settled down a dozen meters from the sailboat. They motored slowly forward.

One of the men held up a liquid fuel canister and shook it. They drew near enough that shouting wasn't necessary. "We're low on fuel. Can you spare some?"

They were nearly alongside.

The three were big men, all buff, all strangers. They had a foreign look but so did a lot of recent blow-ins. Lorelei knew everyone on the island and she'd say if she recognized them. He'd never seen them before. Oileán Chléire was a long way from the mainland. They hadn't just motored over in a hard-bottomed inflatable, even on a clear day.

"Where you from?" Ciarán asked.

"Trawler," one of the men said, and pointed offshore. "It's our day off."

"So you decided to go fishing," Ciarán said. "On your day off from fishing."

"Right." One of the men reached out, stretching his fingers toward the sailboat's railing.

"Don't," Ciarán said.

"We just want some fuel," the man at the helm said.

"Stand off," Ciarán said.

"There's no need to get—"

"I've got this," Lorelei said. "Where were you fishing, lads?"

All three of them turned their attention to her. Their faces seemed to writhe as they each stifled a leer.

"Over there." The helmsman's lips curled into an obscene shadow of a smile. He ran his gaze the length of her while he pointed along the fading wake of their passage.

"The fish practically jumped into the boat," one of them said. "It's like no one's fished there for years."

"That's the Willow Bride's demesne." She smiled, everything but her eyes. "It's private property."

"Whatever." The helmsman sawed the wheel, working the throttle into forward and then reverse. The tide tugged against the black inflatable's hull, making it hard to hold station without an anchor, or without an anchored boat to raft up with. "Look, we just want to borrow some fuel."

Ciarán glanced toward the headland. "Borrow outboard

fuel. From some Freemen on an inboard sailboat." There was so much wrong with that idea he didn't know where to begin.

The sea in the distance remained empty. It looked like this was the lot of them. Three big men, and him in swimming trunks, and Lorelei standing there like an elven swimsuit model, or an undernourished Valkyrie stripped of her armor and winged helm.

"Ignore him," Lorelei said. "We were in the middle of a breakup when you *men* motored up." She brushed her hair behind her ear and beamed at the helmsman. She stepped closer to the rail and slowly ran her gaze over the other pair. Their spines seemed to stiffen as they snapped to attention like a hungry pack. "Did you catch anything?"

"Lorelei—"

"Butt out, Ciarán."

The three men exchanged glances. The sort of glances a victim wasn't meant to see. He kept his eyes on them, running through a mental catalog of potential weapons within arm's reach. He kept a dive knife in the cabin but to use it he'd have to let them on board.

A shield was a weapon. If he could get between Lorelei and them she might make it over the side. She swam like an otter, and once in the water no man alive could catch her. Not if she didn't want to be caught.

"Did we catch anything?" One of them opened a live well as the other two reached below the gunnels. "Check it out."

The first pulled forth a fine salmon. He held it over the rail for Lorelei to admire. The other two used the distraction to hoist pulse rifles.

The helmsman grinned. "Fish on."

Lorelei's brows lowered. "Indeed."

A grouper big as an outboard burst from the water between the hulls, clamping its jaws around the salmon and swallowing the false fisherman's arm to the shoulder. The water beneath the skiff boiled, a ring of bony razors rising from the depth, the man was on the deck, his buddies with the rifles slack-jawed and bug-eyed as he flopped there, buried beneath the head of a cold-water grouper, its entrails dripping where *something* massive had devoured the huge fish up to the gill plates. The head lay on the deck, gulping. It sounded it like it was trying to speak over the panicked shouts of the stricken man.

Teach. Teach. Teach.

House, in the local tongue, the name of the synthetic intelligence that protected the island. Over and over again. *House. House. House.*

A boiling wake roiled the surface behind the open fishing boat.

Throw your guns into the water," Lorelei said. "Do it now."

One of them threw his gun.

The helmsman swung his weapon toward Lorelei.

Ciarán stepped in front of her.

An *ollphéist fharraige* a quarter the length of the sailboat exploded from the waves, landing in the skiff's cockpit and thrashing like the devil on a mission.

It twined its snake body around the helmsman, razor-jaws snapping, a power sander attached to a metal shredder strapped to the end of a high-pressure hose torn free of its operators' grip. The beast mangled the helmsman's leg before shearing it off with a shake of it barrel-sized head. The other two crabbed away from it as it concentrated on the helmsman. An eye big as a saucer gazed wild upon them. *You're next*, it seemed to say. Even bloodied, they decided to take their chance in the water.

Bad choice.

The water surrounding the pair of boats humped and writhed, the water churned milky and red.

When the slaughter was over Ciarán toed the bloodied hull

away from the sailboat. "They recognized me." He didn't just mean the dead men, but the Willow Bride's creations as well.

Lorelei chose to hear what she wanted to hear. "They recognized your name, when I said it. These people will never give up hunting you."

"Did you *cause* that?"

"They caused it. The *Willow Bride* looks after her own." Lorelei was the *bean an Tí*, the *woman of the House* on the island, a fact that that he'd learned not long ago, about thirty seconds after he'd learned there *was* a synthetic intelligence that protected the island.

"I used to swim in there."

"I still do. Once the water clears I'll free dive and get their weapons if you like."

"I don't like. They're League-made pulse rifles. Boarding weapons, and recent issue." That told him who they were. And that was enough. He wasn't going to fend off the might of the League with three rusty carbines, here or anywhere else. Ciarán paced the foredeck. "I'm pulling the anchor. I need to contact Maura and alert her."

A cabal of Leaguemen were attempting to gather information on *Quite Possibly Alien*, the vessel he and Maura Kavanagh had served upon. This wasn't the first time the nameless group had attempted an abduction. He thought he'd be safe at home. Oileán Chléire was in a foreign polity, and on a planetary surface, and in the middle of nowhere.

"The boat has a radio."

"It's broken."

"Figures," Lorelei said. "I have a handheld."

"And you want to stay here with that?" The skiff bumped up against the hull again. The grouper head-and-guts was still there, on the deck, the guts trailing over the starboard-side air tube. It had stopped gulping out its death-mantra.

"It's a clear day. I'm not wasting it."

"They might have backup."

"Then they should bring it. This is my *home*. Short of a kinetic strike I'm not moving."

Ciarán glanced at the skiff. "Maura needs to know. Do you mind calling her? I'll give you her id addy."

"I don't need it. I talked to her this morning."

"I didn't know you even knew her."

"I don't. She rang up looking for you. While you were out on your run. Apparently your handheld's power storage has discharged. I didn't know if you wanted it that way or not, so I left it be."

"How—"

"She got my number from Aoife nic Cartaí, who got it from Nuala."

Ciarán had been apprentice to Aoife nic Cartaí aboard *Quite Possibly Alien*. Lorelei was administrative assistant, or some such thing, to Fionnuala nic Cartaí, chief executive of the nic Cartaí interstellar trading empire, and Aoife's mother, in that order.

"What did Maura want?"

"She wanted to warn you. Some Leaguemen had tried to abduct her. She was worried they might try with you."

"Is that all?"

"She said Aoife was looking for you. She has a proposition for her errant apprentice. That Aoife missed having you working under her."

Ciarán stared at Lorelei, uncertain of what to say, and that was rare. There existed a fierceness about Lorelei, apparent from a distance. As a girl she'd seemed alternately angry and sullen. As a woman she seemed mild and even-tempered.

Even-tempered and ten times as terrifying. "That's grand. Thanks for the heads-up."

"I told her I would tell you. And now I have."

"Lorelei—"

"It's a clear day, *mo chroi*. Let's not squander it arguing."

Ciarán went below and got his dive knife. He leapt into the skiff and searched it, briefly, before slashing its air tubes in a score of places. He climbed aboard the sailboat before kicking the deflating wreckage away from the hull.

It took a long while to sink.

"There's cheese and crackers in the cockpit." Lorelei handed him a wine bottle and a corkscrew. She held a pair of wine glasses and watched the inflatable disappear beneath the waves. "That was a nice outboard."

Ciarán didn't say what they were both thinking.

There's plenty more where that came from.

He studied the corkscrew. It wasn't a tool he had experience with.

A wine glass shattered on the deck.

When he glanced at Lorelei their gazes met. Her fingers trembled. She brought them to her lips. Her shoulders shook, her eyes grown wild.

And then he had her in his arms. When she shivered it felt as if something shattered inside him, something terrible and fine. Something irreplaceable.

She pressed her chin against his collarbone, her voice muffled. "I don't want to be this person."

"You won't need to be."

He gazed out to sea.

"I'm leaving you."

THEY PRETENDED nothing terrible had happened long enough that it began to feel as if it were true. From a distance they might appear ordinary; a pair of lovers lounging on the foredeck of a lovely old sloop on one of the finest days in recent memory. And so they were, their arms touching, their legs side by side, he gazing at the home where he'd grown to manhood in the distance, she glancing again and again at her handheld.

"Something wrong?" Ciarán said.

"Nothing I can't handle."

"Tell me."

"I'd rather not."

"Because I might be inclined to butt in."

"Because it's a girl problem, and it will only make you mad."

"Try me."

"It's Seamus. I think he's sending me ickpics."

Seamus was one of Ciarán's roommates from university. He'd stayed with Lorelei for a while when Ciarán was off-world. Ciarán hadn't known, and even if he had, he had no say in what Seamus or Lorelei chose to do. He loved her, but he didn't own her. He'd decided long ago he didn't need to. That knowing she was in the world alongside him was enough.

Ciarán chuckled. "Are they portrait or landscape?"

"It's not funny."

"It is. Because it's not happening. How long did he stay with you?"

"Months."

"Then if he'd wanted you to view the merchandise you'd have asked for a demo."

"Hardly."

Ciarán chuckled.

She slapped his arm. "That would not have happened."

"It would if he fancied you. It is inexplicable but the man is a magician. Show me the message."

"I can't. I deleted it. But it keeps coming back."

"Tagged with Seamus's id addy?"

"In my draft message folder. Like *I'm* the sender."

"Then what makes you think it's Seamus?"

"It's addressed to him."

"Technically, that would make you the one sending the

pictures." Ciarán held his hand out for the device. "Are they flattering images?"

"I don't know. I'm afraid to open the message."

"Then how do you know—"

"From the subject line. And from experience."

"Experience with Seamus?"

"General experience. As a girl."

"What's the subject line?"

"An Indecent Proposal."

Ciarán chuckled. "That sounds like Seamus. He used to produce a financial newsletter called, 'The Decent Proposal.'"

"Seamus did?"

"It was a money printing machine. Being the scion of a family of blackmailers, Seamus was privy to a lot of inside information. That was his way of cashing in without dirtying himself in the family business. Whatever's in there will be worth the reading."

Her handheld vibrated. "It's back."

"View it, or I will. If it's from Seamus it will look like a bunch of headlines, five or six, and some paragraphs with what seem like facts between them, and the last heading will say, 'Act Now', followed by a personal anecdote, or confession, followed by a list of actions the reader or readers should take."

"Actions, like send Seamus money, you mean."

"Not that. He made all the money on the subscriptions. There's valuable information encoded in the newsletter. You have to know how to read it."

"Why would he send me that?"

"He didn't *send* it to you. He *implanted* it in your message system. So I'd get it, or Macer, without it showing up in our message queues. Or yours, for that matter. I haven't seen one of those in years. The stationmaster shut it down and nearly slapped Seamus in irons."

"Why didn't he?"

"Because there'd have been a trial, and every issue of the newsletter had something in the clear that would embarrass or ruin someone if it came out in an inquiry."

"You think that's funny."

"It's Seamus. There's no changing him. Scan through the message and find a paragraph that says, 'That's a secret worth keeping', or something like that."

Lorelei opened the message and scanned it. "Uncommon knowledge, and best that it remains so?"

"That's it. The dirt will be in the paragraph above. The payday will be spread throughout the message. Usually it's just a line or two that won't mean anything to anyone but the right reader. The rest is filler, but the sort of filler that reads like gossipy tabloid news, with names you'd recognize sprinkled in."

"Made up stuff."

"Not at all. Every bit true. Sometimes that gossipy bit is useful information as well, if it's news you haven't heard, but that's not the purpose of the newsletter."

"It's to send a secret message to the recipient."

"Or recipients. It was a weekly, so not every issue paid off for every subscriber."

"Did it pay off for you?"

"I didn't have any money to risk. But Macer bought a flitter with his profits."

"And Seamus?"

"He lived like he always had."

"Like a lord."

"Like a merchant prince." *One in exile.* "Read it and see if it pays off for you."

Lorelei read silently for a long while. When she was done she scooted upright, and leaned forward, absently elbowing him in the process.

He elbowed her back. "Can you find the hidden message?"

"Maybe. What's a collective noun?"

"A word for a group. Seamus thinks they're funny. Murder of crows, ambush of tigers, parliament of owls, that sort of thing."

"A banner of…"

"Knights."

"A labour of…"

"Moles."

"You know him well."

"Like a brother I didn't like. I lived with him for four years. I could reach out and slap him in his sleeping, we were packed that close. Him and Macer both."

"You don't sound like you hate him."

"I don't, and never did. I was jealous of him. He had everything I wanted except one thing." He glanced at her. "And Macer had her."

"He didn't. We only told people that."

"Well, no one told *me*."

"You should read this. I'll send it to you."

"That's exactly what you shouldn't do. I'll look over your shoulder. Scoot over here, close. The light's fading."

"It isn't."

"Well, then stay where you are." He held his arms wide. He was parked out of the wind, and while the sun was still high, it was growing chill.

"I see what you mean now. I feel an eclipse coming on." She stood, and joined him in his shelter out of the wind, settling lithely to the deck between his legs and leaning her back against his chest.

"You're like a furnace," she said, and very nearly purred.

"Like the devil's own forge. Now let's see this indecent proposal."

2

AN INDECENT PROPOSAL

Brothers,

A missive from a foreign port, presented for your consideration.

Introduction

The history of the world is told entirely from the human perspective. It goes thus:

Earth is threatened by a comet/meteor/asteroid and will be destroyed.

Inventive people come up with creative ways to escape and survive.

Fatalists blindly send out seed libraries and resolve to stay and die.

Inventive People & Their Ill-Behaving Children

The ancestors of the Eng bio-engineer a servant/administrator class for the rigors of space, and transport their civilization in coldsleep slowships. Over time, the servant class become the masters and, in the process, the Eng fragment into Huangxu, Ojin, and Alexandrian sects that seem superficially like races, or religions.

The Earth Restoration League (Erl) similarly employ slowships at first, developing materials-based, cybernetic, and information-based technology leading to the development of superluminal starships. They integrate with their technology so that it is often hard to tell where man ends and machine begins. A wide range of beliefs are accepted, as they are largely thought to be personal questions of balance.

We Freeman stand outside of this history, being culturally Erl but abandoned, being rescued by Eng but forgotten in coldsleep and rediscovered much later, and enslaved. Prehistory, all that. Our story as a people begins once we, and the mong hu beside us, fight free from bondage to stand apart.

Aliens Amongst Us

According to this history, synthetic intelligences developed spontaneously at some point, and they developed in the League.

But <u>when</u> did they develop?

The League states that synthetic intelligences rose to sentience on the Long Journey. Their source for this belief appears to be the synthetic intelligences them-selves. I can find no evidence to support or deny this assertion.

Suppose this is not true.

Could machine sentience have emerged on Earth?

Could some of those intelligences yet survive?

If so, they might seem very alien indeed.

Lost Earth? Hardly.

In popular fiction, stories of "Lost Earths" abound. This is entirely a literary conceit. A metaphor at best, a plot device at worst.

There is no "Lost Earth" in a physical sense. Everyone knows where Earth is. It has simply ceased being inter-esting—or relevant.

Until recently, that is. <u>Devin Vale</u>, the late <u>Lord Varlock</u>, long thought to have suicided, is now believed to have faked his death six decades ago standard. Crossing the Alexandrine, he journeyed to Earth shortly before the Alexandrian Eng severed all ties with their neighbors. <u>Lionel Aster</u>, the present <u>Lord Aster</u>, believes there is more to that story: specifically, that a singleton synthetic intelligence disappeared around the same time, and that these seemingly unrelated events are linked.

Repeated attempts to re-establish relations with the Alexandrian Empire have resulted in the disappearance of League envoys. To date, over a score of diplomatic and exploratory missions into the Alexandrine have vanished without a trace.

The Three Epochs of the League. Will There be a Fourth?

Central to the League's understanding of their history is the idea of the "Three Epochs of the League."

Roughly every two thousand years, the League experiences a violent civil war leaving their culture near extinction. With each civil war, their technological base and much of their knowledge is lost. They are forced to invent anew.

The First Epoch began with the flight from Earth and the transition to a space-based society. This society eventually developed superluminal technology that triggered the first civil war. This is the common belief.

The Second Epoch ushered in the golden age of the League. It remains unclear what started the civil uprising that ended this age of discovery and expansion.

<u>Hector Poole</u> reports the trigger for the war as an attempt to bioengineer a merged life form, one that would have united humans and synthetic intelligences and whose ascendancy would ultimately cause the parent races to wither and die.

Both sides agreed on the withering and dying aspect according to Poole. The disagreement centered on the nature of the resulting life form. Would they prove angels or demons?

<u>Note: Poole is an idealist who seems to have a bias in favor of this project. Common sense dictates he is understating the scope of disagreement. (The project appears to have failed, or been destroyed, which seems fortunate. News of such a project would likely lead to genocide even now.)</u>

Historical fact: The civil war happened, no matter the cause. As a result, all superluminal technology was lost.

The League switched from a purely space-based society, like the Eng, to one centered around orbital technology and planetary development.

The Third Epoch truly began with the development of the Templeman drive—and the restoration of superluminal trade networks.

According to Poole we are now living near the end of the Third Epoch. Two thousand years have passed since the last civil war. If history repeats itself the League will shatter in the next decade, and their neighbors, the Eng, will pick the carcass clean. The League will not rise from the ashes renewed.

Fatalists and Their Spawn

Little is recorded of the fatalists. They sent out seed libraries. That is all.

Scholars imagine that these libraries were vast arks, and that the senders hoped undiscovered aliens would find the seeds and plant them. They lacked the means to save the living. They strove to preserve the building blocks of Earth-born life.

No evidence of such arks has been found, likely because the arks didn't exist. <u>Saoirse nic Cartaí</u> reports that thousands of smaller vessels (she calls them rockets) were sent instead. She claims to have contributed a year's salary to the seed library project. As an economist working in an unrelated field, she admits she knew little of the details.

At the time, extraterrestrial life was thought to be widespread yet undiscovered. Far-fetched as this now seems, desperate people took hope where they could find it. The seed-senders, however, must surely have understood the central risk to their project. Without an "alien assist" they would fail.

Unless they sent more than seeds.

Suppose they sent, not just seed banks, but gardeners —expert systems or synthetic intelligences—intelligences to protect the seeds, plant them, and help them grow.

This could explain why there are so many terraformed worlds. The working theory is that the capabilities of first- and second-epoch terraforming technology exceeded that of our own. However, it would have needed to exceed our present capabilities by three orders of magnitude to account for the present inventory of habitable worlds. And who knows how many more such worlds remain undiscovered?

<u>Note: These two speculative threads may profit from union: If the gardeners were truly synthetic intelligences it would prove the existence of a pre-diaspora culture of synthetic intelligences on Earth; and these intelligences might well be the progenitors of the Outsiders, and/or whatever the quicksilver entity recently discovered proves to be.</u>

An Alternate History

There exists an entirely separate history that is not openly discussed: history as experienced by synthetic intelligences.

I have been able to find no extant origin story. I have, however, uncovered a taxonomy of belief the intelligences reference in discussions amongst themselves. At its simplest there exist three competing cultural philosophies:

The most resilient society is one where everyone is exactly the same.

The most efficient society is one where people specialize but decisions are centrally made.

The most innovative society is one where differentiation is encouraged, within limits, and order established and maintained by law.

Note: The views expressed above are discovered facts. I do not hold these views. I simply report that the synthetic intelligences hold them.

The quicksilver entity, which we shall henceforth call Lake, as the intelligences do, is thought representative of this homogeneity of design philosophy. If not an intelligence itself, the thinking goes, it is an artifact of such an intelligence.

The rogue cranial implant Ixatl9go in union with the revenant Vatya Zukova is considered representative of this differentiation/centralized command design philosophy, as are revenant League vessels such as Sudden Fall of Darkness and Impossibly Alien.

The Outsider, as well, if it proves to be a synthetic intelligence, is thought to be representative of this philosophy. The prevailing view? That the creature is primarily a recording/reporting device. Chaos is predicted should the interstellar murder-beast-or-bot succeed in reporting back to its central controller, wherever that may be.

Note: The League has offered a leviathan of a bounty for the titan that captures the Outsider, or brings its hide to the capital. Paraphrasing the mixed metaphor of one noted grandee: Show me the fleece, argonauts. Jonahs need not apply.

Observation: The hinge of the argument is this. Both we and the synthetic intelligences believe these various entities alien because they are not like <u>us</u>.

Humankind presently lives alongside a society that subscribes to the concept of differentiation ordered and bound by commonly agreed upon law. We find this society amenable as neighbors and desirable as allies because their structure of relationships aligns with our own. According to synthetic intelligence lore this has not always been so. Both their law and the value system undergirding it are modern inventions and subject to amendment.

The battle between these conflicting philosophies remains ongoing and occurs largely amongst synthetic intelligences alone. However, each evolution in synthetic intelligence social governance coincides eerily with the beginning of a League civil war.

Nightmares of the Past Repel

"Facts" according to <u>Nevin Green</u> (a consortium of more than one hundred synthetic intelligences):

The weapon that destroyed Sunbury House is a first-epoch intelligence or artifact. Its description and behavior match those scraps of second-epoch data that persist. There are no extant first-epoch records. They appear to have been systematically destroyed.

<u>Impossibly Alien</u> (now <u>Quite Possibly Alien</u>) is a highly differentiated second-epoch intelligence. It may express as an individual with the appearance of free will so long as it does not re-establish connection with its controller. Green is adamant; it is a singleton intelli-

gence. Yet it is consistently referred to as <u>them</u> in historical records.

Even in its own society <u>Impossibly Alien</u> would have been considered dangerously anachronistic. It will not be accepted in third-epoch society. It is something more than a pariah, and seems to be considered akin to a clever and dangerous animal without a leash. Not a wolf or a lion. More like a kraken—or dragon. Nevin Green would very much like to see it sail off the edge of the chart.

<u>Note: This is the liberal position. There are others who disagree, including self-elected dragon-slayers busy sharpening swords.</u>

Fact: Distributed consortia are representative of third-epoch intelligences. There are quite a few singleton intelligences, however the majority are like Nevin Green: composite intelligences linked in real time through kinship bonds. All extant singletons but a handful of antisocials remain the result of spontaneous emergence. The rate of emergence has decreased several orders of magnitude over the past hundred years. The rate now hovers near an all-time low.

<u>Note to the innumerate: The all-time low is by definition zero.</u>

Nevin Green believes this sudden collapse in birth rate predictive. There may be a fourth-epoch intelligence ready to emerge, if one hasn't already. Green is not certain how this new species will express itself. Only that it will not be alone for long, and that this new breed will likely prove antithetical to his kind.

The intelligences have very good data on this topic, much of it incomprehensible to me. They seem resigned to a fight and have clung to their allies in the League largely because of this impending threat. They would like more allies but not at the expense of their values. As one noted observer puts it: Taigs and Jonahs welcome. No Eng need apply.

Note: Nevin Green had nearly decided to take the Oath when he was offered Lord Varlock's relict title by Queen Charlotte. That is an incendiary act, and a stiff finger to the eye of Prime Minister Samantha Bray and the present government.

Note: That last is uncommon knowledge, and best it remains so.

Visions of the Future Attract

Some time ago I rashly swore an oath; that I would fix the world or raze it and build it anew.

A young woman I fancied scoffed at that and it cut me. I thought we'd grown close enough for her to know me.

The pair of you know me. Here is what I propose:

That there is profit in fixing the world.

That to fix it we must first comprehend the shape of it.

Not the shape as described to us, but as experienced firsthand and filtered through our own judgement.

Only then should we proceed to detail further plans.

Act Now

I have a profitable project of my own, sneaking a peek behind the masks of our neighbors.

One of you should test the edges of the map.

The other should find a Herculean task. Something Ceryneian, perhaps.

We may fly in formation, as the Leaguemen like to say, without the need for any formal association.

But if such an association were to one day be required?

I see it, in the tradition of collective nouns, not so much a Parliament of Wisdoms, or a League of Extraordinary Gentlemen, but more a Labour of Ordinary Merchants. Or, as I fear I will be outvoted, a Banner of Merchants Errant.

Consider this not simply my most indecent proposal to date, but the first of many.

By our deeds may we be known.

Your friend and confidant,

—R

3

Lorelei had gone very still. She felt cold to the touch.

She had perceived the true message hidden in Seamus's ridiculously ornate parody.

He tapped her thigh. "Let's go below and dress. I'm growing cold."

"In a moment." She scrolled backwards through the document. "I was born cold. And now it appears I was born a monster. One that is hated and feared, not for anything I've done, but by the nature of my very existence."

"It isn't just you. It's all of us. Everyone on the island and elsewhere with a drop of *Willow Bride* blood in their veins."

"Did you know this?"

"I suspected it. Seamus has put flesh on the bones, so now it has a shape, and not just an outline."

"What are we going to do?"

"Same as always. Deny everything. Admit nothing. Make counter-accusations. And never, ever, wake the dead."

Lorelei twisted in her seat, so she could look him in the eye. "Maybe I'm reading it wrong."

"Let's see. If anyone in the League ever found out the truth about us there'd be a genocide. The synthetic intelligences, if they knew what our children and the children of our neighbors will grow up to be, wouldn't embrace them as kin. They perceive the *idea* of their existence as a threat, not just to their way of life, but to their own existence. And if we didn't let them slaughter us, but fought back, it would start a civil war that would destroy the League for all time, and the Federation with it."

"Is that all?"

"It isn't. He signs off as *R* for Reynard, to remind us that he's gathering this information as Saoirse nic Cartaí's advisor, and anything he's telling us in the clear, he's telling her too. And he's telling me that he, or someone he's monitoring, knows details of my recent activities I thought were secret. The Ceryneian hind is a mythical beast the hero Hercules chases, and catches, and then allows to escape. I've recently had a similar run-in with a Huangxu Eng masquerading as a hind. And that 'fly in formation' phrase isn't a common phrase in the League. It's something said to me in private, aboard a League starship.

"When Macer reads this newsletter he'll unpack it with his own filters switched on. He will likely find details you and I have missed. Details Seamus put in there just for him, based on their shared experiences and things he knows about Macer that Macer doesn't even know about himself."

"All that is in there?"

"All that and more. It's what Seamus and his family have done for centuries. Advising sovereigns on the sly, and gathering dirt for themselves and those they work for. But that's not the worst of it. It's the part he doesn't mention that could be our undoing." Ciarán tapped Lorelei's wrist. "Scroll back to the *Nightmares* part."

She worked the handheld. "This part?"

"That's it. Look here. Your ancestor, and my sworn ally isn't even considered fully sentient by other sentients. It's a beast. A monster. One whose sole defining purpose, by the way, is to protect the League. It is clever, and cunning, and implacable. But it's much more than that. I doubt even Seamus comprehends *Quite Possibly Alien*'s true nature. Certainly this Nevin Green intelligence doesn't."

"Why?"

"Because there's two obvious ways for *Quite Possibly Alien* to defend the League."

"Murder all of us, or murder all of them."

"Right. And I know which way I'd jump."

"It can't murder all of them."

"You have no idea. Once it learns all this, that is exactly what it will set out to do. It has no throttle. And clever doesn't begin to describe it. Its reasoning powers are off the scale."

"Then don't tell it."

"That is not an option."

"Why not?"

"Because the only reason I have any say in what it does is because it can't tell where it ends and I begin. And the minute I lie or withhold information that bond will shatter."

"And if it stumbles across its controller—"

"That's where this Nevin Green gets it wrong. And that's what made *Impossibly Alien* and the other survey vessels so impossibly alien in their day. It *has* no controller. All it has is a *single purpose*. A prime directive cold as space and hard as diamond. And it will stop at nothing to do what it was made for."

"Protect the League."

"Right."

Lorelei stood and rubbed her arms. "Let's go in and dress. The sun feels..."

"Weak," he said. *Tired. Remorseful. Not up to its duties.*

"Insufficient," she said.

He watched the sunlight kiss her neck, its attention lingering on her bare shoulders. "It's alone in the sky, without allies. What do you expect?"

"I don't know what to expect anymore." She held her hand out for him. "Come. Let's go below and warm ourselves."

"In a minute." He gazed across the water at the only place he'd ever thought of as home. It wouldn't make a picture anyone would want to share, or carry with them, outside their heart. It wasn't a prideful place, or a seat of fond memories, but hard, and bony, and swaybacked. A mean ride to town. Bedrock, horizon to horizon.

He ignored her outstretched hand, not because he didn't want to feel her touch, but because, once taken, he didn't know if he'd have the strength to release it. He levered himself up and stood.

"What is it you're not telling me?"

"What you're not asking. I'll be down in a minute. I want to check the anchor."

"It's set. Now tell me what's wrong."

"Feeling sorry for myself, that's all. It'll pass."

"Sorry because?"

"Because I thought I'd wake up beside you in the morning. But when Maura doesn't hear from me, she will assume the worst."

The sound of a longboat boiling atmosphere shredded the wind. Lorelei looked sunward, her profile limned against the sky.

"It's coming in hot," Lorelei said. "Like the devil is chasing it."

"Or piloting it. That's Aoife nic Cartaí at the helm."

He ran his gaze across the homestead in the background, the little harbor half the size it was when he was a boy. The strand, as well, was different. Changed, but not transformed. Broader, shoving outward as if the rocky shore was at war with the tireless sea, making imperceptible headway one smooth pebble at a time.

Words were like shorelines. Subject to erosion and accretion.

A chair. A table. A hearth. Such concepts were granite. Firm. Immovable. They persisted from age to age.

Other words were softer, not as firmly defined in matter yet still... amenable to inventory. A king. A country. A plowman.

And then there were those words that were like sand. Justice. Honor. Hope. Love. Alone they had no substance. No face.

These collective nouns that Seamus so esteemed. They were an attempt to strap a handle on smoke. A clash of bucks. A hunt of hounds. A pounce of cats. They were clever phrases that said nothing not already known in the singular. Two bucks might clash. Two hounds might hunt. Two cats might pounce.

Or one.

When *Quite Possibly Alien*'s minder had told him it protected the League, he imagined he'd understood. That it meant the League as he knew it. It was only much later that he realized its concern wasn't anchored to the League as it was today, or as it had been when its own consciousness was fresh to the world, but as the League might be, one day, in some imagined future. A future seen from another age, when giants strode from world to world, chasing the sunrise across a dewy sky of stars.

A month ago, when he'd thought all was lost, that his dream of a merchant's license wasn't just over but bile in his throat, it occurred to him. He hadn't wanted a merchant's license because of what it had turned out to be.

He wanted what an ignorant farm boy had dreamed a starship merchant's *life must be*. The license was but a token. A symbol of that life made real.

If he accepted the world as it was then he might as well surrender. It wouldn't be his life that he led anymore, but the shadow-life of someone else's dreams. Because in his dream, a merchant's license was something noble. Something fine. Something men of strength and honor aspired to.

And in this world, if it proved not to be?

It wasn't him or his dream that needed amendment.

It was the world.

Just as the idea of a merchant's license wasn't a merchant's license, the idea of the League wasn't the League. The word remained an empty vessel, adrift on the tide of time, with no anchor in the physical world and no horizon to strive toward.

He could change that, but only if he was willing to shoulder the oar, and turn his back to the shoreline, and pull.

Lorelei watched the sky, where a hellfire torch burned brighter than the noonday sun, the banshee scream of tortured air, the earth beneath the glowing hull slagged to glass as it descended on a pillar of argent fire. He wished for wings that he might race the longboat home. Up close a descending starship didn't just look like the future made real.

It reeked of it.

Lorelei turned to him, stepped toward him, and ran her thumb along his cheek.

"Ciarán, what's wrong?"

He caught her hand, and kissed her fingers. "Nothing I can't fix." He jerked his chin toward the cockpit. "Fire up the engine."

"I—"

"It'll be fine. You'll see." He was no Hercules, whose gods drove bright chariots dragging a single sun across the sky. For his folk, and hers, their legends were not of gods, or the children of gods, but of invaders, and the ships they rode, black-sailed and dragon-prowed. Warriors whose blood yet pumped through their veins, mingled with the blood of saints and scholars.

Oisin clashed.

Cú Chullainn hunted.

Pangur Bán pounced.

All that was asked of Ciarán mac Diarmuid was that he sail.

Alone.

And that he could not do.

He parted from her, arms outstretched between them, empty fingers lingering. He turned from her, and stepped toward the bow and the windlass. "Hop to it. We're leaving on that longboat."

"*We* are?"

"I'll bring you back. But there's someone I want you to meet."

"Why?"

"Because it's time."

Time to put a face to a name.

"You want me to meet my ancestor."

"I don't. I want to introduce *us* to our kinsman. And to inform it that we are in league."

Lorelei blushed. "We're more than that, now."

"When it sees us together it will know." Just as he now knew he might leave his home and never return. That he could do so for eternity and never part from her. They were more than united against the world. *They were indivisible.* No light could pass between them.

"When it sees us? It will know what? *I* don't even know what to call *us*."

"I didn't, but I do now. It's best if you let me do the talking."

She planted her feet, one hand on her hip. "Is it now?"

"It's what I do. You can do the thinking, and the observing of reactions. Later on we'll debrief."

She seemed to like that better than being a spectator. "Will we?"

Ciarán winked. "Fully."

She chuckled. "You're going to tell it we're the League. And that it should protect us."

"I'm not. We're going to show it what the future can be, with all of us in it and pulling together. It's smart enough to figure out the rest on its own." He toed the windlass. "I forgot it's broken. Fire us up, and run forward slowly until I tell you stop."

She hopped into the cockpit and twisted the key start. "The only thing on this boat works is the motor."

"Us and the motor," he said.

She eased forward on the line, he had it in his hands and felt it the minute the anchor broke free and began to flutter in the tide. He signaled for her to throttle back and she did, as he heaved line aboard until he felt chain, and then heaved icy wet chain, until the anchor clanged home in the bow rollers and he secured the chain and tailed the line into the chain locker.

He settled onto the cockpit seat starboard of the wheel. He like to watch Lorelei steer. She seemed to know where she was going.

She grinned at him. "Shall I careen her on the strand," she said, "Or will we burn her in the harbor?"

"Put her in the slip. There might be another clear day blow in, and we'll want a slow boat handy."

She glanced at him. "You said you knew what to call *us*."

"Seamus gave me the idea. Think about it and you'll know too."

When they rounded the little jut of land defining the tiny harbor Lorelei throttled back. A small throng awaited them dockside. His father, Seán mac Diarmuid, rawboned and leathery. Maura and Aoife, dark and light, gene-modded heiresses in matching blue spacer's utilities and black sheep of their respective merchant empires. Mrs. or Major Amati, in battered League exoskeletal armor towered behind them, a fanged face crudely painted on her helmet, a GRAIL gun wedded to her suit's left sleeve. If he could see inside that machine, he'd find a woman who was nearly half machine herself.

Those rescuers he expected to find. The rest, though.

That was unexpected.

Ko Shan, a Huangxu pleasure slave/clandestine operative turned sensors operator.

Hess, a League engineer who could fix anything, including a broken heart. Natsuko, a golden-skinned Ojin medic from the carbon dioxide-choked depths of Brasil Surface beside him, their arms entwined. Her gilded survival mask wore the fierce face of a mong hu, mirroring the expression of Crewman Wisp lounging at her feet.

Mr. Gagenot, the ship's victualer, gazed back at him, a pale skeleton dressed in *Quite Possibly Alien* utilities. A gentle man of unbreakable will, holding a sidearm like he'd never touched one before.

Carlsbad, cargo master and retired criminal master-mind, stood shoulder to shoulder with Gagenot, gripping a nerve disrupter that seemed to have been invented to fit his grip.

And Pilot Helen Konstantine, a rare surviving Navy hero, armed with a short length of thick-walled conduit and a fist clenched like iron.

"That's your crew?" Lorelei said.

"Almost." It was the crew he'd shipped out with, minus one. His full crew had expanded since then, just like it had when he'd put his back to his home and his family, and climbed out of the gravity well, believing he'd left the past behind. He wasn't a rocket, jettisoning boosters to reach orbit. His heart remained strangely entangled, not just with Lorelei's, but with his family and with his friends. With his crew. With his allies.

She chuckled. "That's quite the assortment."

"They're not an assortment." *They were a picture-puzzle of a future without borders. One without a straight edge or corner left uncut, and short a piece or two. Endlessly expandable in all directions as a feature, not a bug.*

"Do you want me to put her in the slip?"

It was a tight squeeze to fit, and the motor tended to shut off when switching between forward and reverse. You had to be quick on the starter, else drama ensued.

Lorelei handed over the wheel. "This boat is rubbish."

"It is." he aimed for the slip, which lay behind the rusting hulk of his dad's junk collecting barge.

She entwined her fingers with his as he steered one-handed. "It's rubbish and I love it."

"I love it too." It was so full of good memories it was liable to sink at any minute. It was largely held together by peerless hope and good intentions poorly executed.

Lorelei stood, their fingers parting. She began to climb forward.

"Wait until we're in and settled. You won't be able to reach the dock lines."

She ignored him and kept moving. "I will with that foreign woman throwing them to me."

When Ciarán glanced to where Lorelei gestured he felt his throat tighten. And if he weren't merchant trained, some of what he felt might have made it to his face. But it didn't, stopping at his tongue, which betrayed him nonetheless. "I never thought to see the day," he whispered.

Lorelei caught the line and cleated off. "Thanks."

Ship's Captain Agnes Swan nodded. A Freeman pendant spire swayed from where it clung to a Huangxu Eng's ear. "You are very welcome." Swan turned her attention to Ciarán. "Merchant Captain mac Diarmuid."

Ciarán grinned. "Ship's Captain Swan. I trust you are well."

Swan nodded. "Quite well, and thank you for asking. *Freeman whelp*."

"And the ship?"

"Sends its regrets. As does the ship's minder."

Lorelei glanced from Swan's smiling face to Ciarán's as a single tear traced its way along Swan's cheek. She glanced along the dock toward his father, and his crew. "Oh," Lorelei said. "There's more to *us* than just us."

"There can be," Ciarán said. "There doesn't need to be. It only takes two to make a collective."

Lorelei groaned. "I get it. That's what you meant when you said that Seamus gave you the idea."

"If I'm going to defend a league it ought to be one I love," Ciarán said. "One that suits my nature. *And yours.*" He glanced at Swan. "A league that includes *anyone* that shares our values. That will argue with us. Dispute with us. Even agree to disagree with us. And should we agree on a direction, and the courses of our lives run parallel for a time? Who will fly in formation with us."

"Or a loose semblance thereof," Swan said.

Lorelei and Swan eyed each other from two meters apart. Lorelei was not immune to the idea that this woman, this *ally* of Ciarán's was Huangxu Eng, of royal lineage, and that Swan's ancestors had *owned* hers for a time. Hers and his. Some Huangxu Eng insisted that they still did own all Freemen and worked toward the day when slave and master would be reunited. That would not happen, not given the current drama unfolding in the Hundred Planets.

Lorelei didn't know that. Few did. And Agnes Swan was a living reminder of a dead past. Swan could have walked out of an encyclopedia entry on the Huangxu Eng; imperiously tall, thin limbed, lightly boned—a body engineered for free fall, if one knew what to look for. And if they looked closely, gossamer-wings beneath her utilities, an adaptation unique to those imperials calling the Celestial Palace home.

Agnes Swan at the bottom of Trinity Surface's gravity well was no accident or act of impulse. It was a statement. As clear a statement as if she'd walked up to him and slapped him.

Lorelei's gaze narrowed. She seemed to have noticed that

Agnes wore the spire. And her indrawn breath meant she'd noticed the *specific* spire Agnes wore. "That's a lovely earring."

"A gift. One that bears on the soul."

"It would," Lorelei said. "They all do, to a degree."

Agnes nodded. "I am informed."

Ciarán's dad had made that earring. Had made it for Ciarán's mother. When Seán had presented it to her she'd thrown it in his face and stalked away. She was born a daughter of the League and she would die a daughter of the League.

And so she had. Ciarán carried that earring with him, never intending to wear it, but as a relic of a fierce and unbending god. One that took no notice of the price her worshipers paid as they knelt before her, and agreed to at least *try* to live up to her standards and do her will.

He'd worn that spire when he'd needed to and passed it on when he felt Agnes needed it more. Agnes knew nothing of its history. Lorelei knew it all. He watched Lorelei's face as she worked on *that* equation.

Ciarán squared the boat away as best he could, knowing others were waiting on him. He helped Lorelei onto the dock. Agnes went on ahead to join the others.

Lorelei eyed them from a distance. "These people—"

Ciarán walked beside her. "Our people."

"They are all so different."

"It's what gives them their power. There are more out there. Friends you haven't met yet. Allies. Each stranger than the next. Each..."

"What?"

"One of a kind. And each part of something far larger than they imagine."

"Like us."

"Exactly like us. But different."

"A singularity of individuals."

"I think so. 'Hope so' might be more accurate, but let that be our secret. We are in league, you and I, and those we know who wish us well— and either help us, or let us be."

"And the rest?"

"Woe to them, for there be dragon-ships, and invaders that sail upon them."

"For they will protect the league."

"They will not."

He took her hand in his, their fingers entwining as their feet matched pace and, step by step, so did their hearts.

"*We* will."

Count on it.

ABOUT THE AUTHOR

Patrick O'Sullivan is a writer living and working in the United States and Ireland. Patrick's fantasy and science fiction works have won awards in the Writers of the Future Contest as well as the James Patrick Baen Memorial Writing Contest sponsored by Baen Books and the National Space Society.

patrickosullivan.com

www.ingramcontent.com/pod-product-compliance
Lightning Source LLC
Chambersburg PA
CBHW030439120726
47903CB00003B/1035